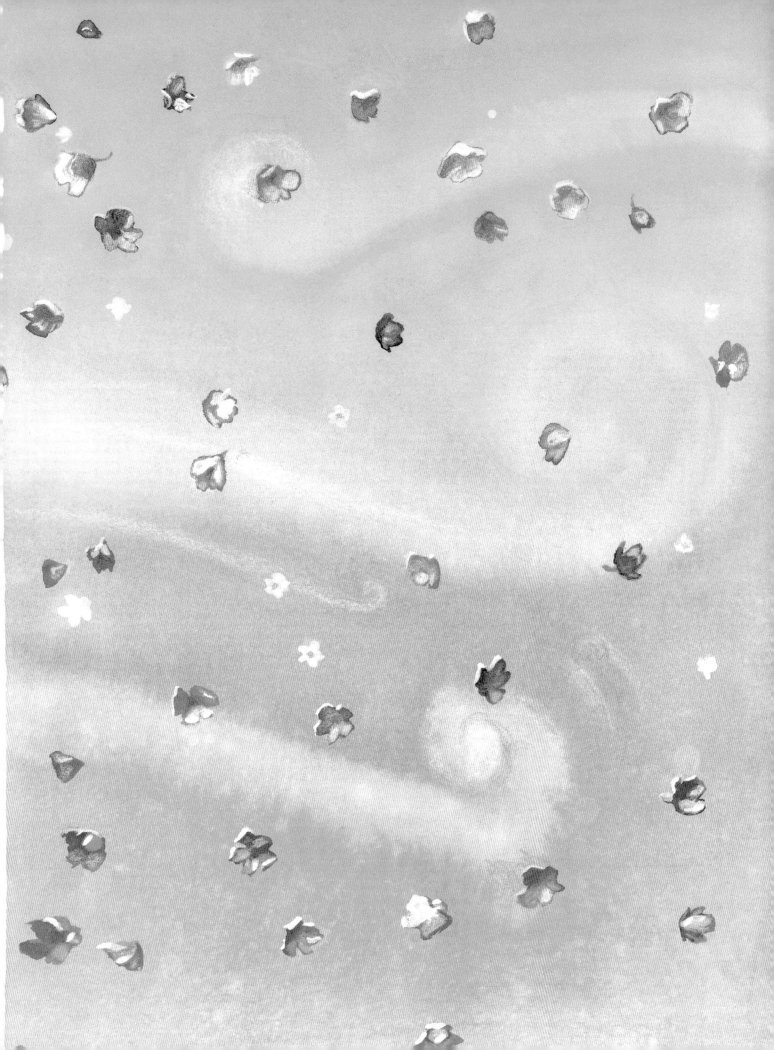

Spring's Sprung

By Lynn Plourde   Illustrated by Greg Couch

Simon & Schuster Books for Young Readers

NEW YORK   LONDON   TORONTO   SYDNEY   SINGAPORE

A Note from the Artist
I work on museum board; it's like a very thick, smooth watercolor paper. I put down many washes of liquid acrylic paint until I get the mood I'm looking for. Then I add details for the faces, clothes, etc. with colored pencils. If the colors aren't bright enough after that, I go back with a small brush and more acrylic to add the finishing touches.

SIMON & SCHUSTER BOOKS FOR YOUNG READERS
An imprint of Simon & Schuster Children's Publishing Division
1230 Avenue of the Americas, New York, New York 10020
Text copyright © 2002 by Lynn Plourde
Illustrations copyright © 2002 by Greg Couch
SIMON & SCHUSTER BOOKS FOR YOUNG READERS is a trademark of Simon & Schuster.
Book design by Paul Zakris
The text of this book is set in 22-point Lomba Medium.
Printed in Hong Kong
10 9 8 7 6 5 4 3 2 1

Library of Congress Cataloging-in-Publication Data

Plourde, Lynn.
Spring's sprung / by Lynn Plourde ; illustrated by Greg Couch.—1st ed.
p. cm.
Summary: Mother Nature rouses her squabbling daughters, March, April, and May, so they can awaken the world and welcome spring.
ISBN 0-689-84229-5
[1. Spring—Fiction. 2. Sisters—Fiction. 3. Stories in rhyme.]
I. Couch, Greg, ill. II. Title.
PZ8.3.P5586922 Sp 2002
[E]—dc21
00-045056

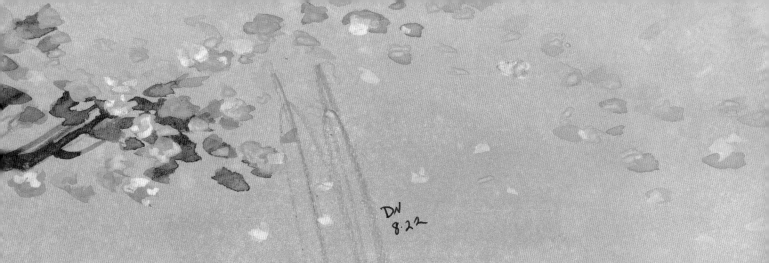

With love to my favorite sibling rivals Cathy, Michael, and Stephen
-L. P.

To Sonya—Spring won't seem quite so beautiful without you.
-G. C.

Mother Earth rouses her daughters—
March, April, and May.
"You must wake the world
to start a new day."

The Spring sisters groan,
don't even budge,
till Mother Earth asks,
"Do you each need a nudge?"

"No," "No," "No,"
they say so quick.
"We'll all be dressed
in a flickety-flick."

March stumbles and tumbles
out of her bed.
Grabs any old thing,
pulls it over her head.

April's more practical.
Finds a one-piece suit.
As long as it's warm,
who cares if it's cute?

May's fussy, yet fast.
Tries to match and mix.
After a dozen tries,
it's the violets she picks.

"First," "First," "First,"
each says with pride.
"Mother, I'm the fastest.
The others lied."

"Mother, Mother!
Look, I'm dressed.
Was I faster
than all the rest?"

Mother Earth smiles
at each of their styles.
"You are the fastest March I ever did see.
And the fastest April I ever did see.
And the fastest May I ever did see."

"Harumph!" "Pooh!" "Dree!"
Each wants to be
the fastest of ALL the three.

Mother Earth warns,
"You're taking too long.
Now stop bickering
and practice your song."

March howls and growls
like a monsoon,
then whiffs and puffs
a quieter tune.

Next, April's song
wets the ground,
as her tinkly, sprinkly
drizzles drip down.

May practices scales,
drill after drill,
then serenades all
with a soprano trill.

"La!" "La!" "La!"
each sings aloud
into Mother's ears—
oh, so proud.

"Mother, Mother,
do I sing the best?
Do I sing better
than all the rest?"

Mother Earth swoons
at each of their tunes.
"You are the best March singer I ever did hear.
And the best April singer I ever did hear.
And the best May singer I ever did hear."

"Harumph!" "Pooh!" "Dree!"
Each wants to be
the best singer of ALL the three.

The sisters squabble
like siblings do.
"Mother loves me
more than she loves you."

"Does not."
"Does too."
"Loves me."
"Not you."
"Sob-sob!"
"Boo hoo!"

Mother Earth shushes her daughters—
March, April, and May.
"Stop this silliness, girls.
Just start the new day."

The Spring sisters
burst into tears,
each holding to hopes,
but fearing their fears.

"Me." "Me." "Me."
"Tell me I'm the one—
your favorite daughter
under the sun."

"Mother, Mother,
do you love me the best?
Do you love me better
than all the rest?"

Mother Earth huddles
her girls in a cuddle.
"Now listen, March, April, May,
and remember what I say."

"A mother's heart
is big enough
to grow and grow,
and stretch and stretch.
The truth—
I love you ALL the best."

"Hooray!" "Whoop!" "Whee!"
"She loves you, you,
and me-e-e-e-e-e-e!"

The Spring sisters
smile with pride,
shouting, "WAKE UP, WORLD!"
skipping side by side.

Spring's Sprung!

A new day's begun.

After waking the world,
time to wake one more girl.
So, March, April, and May
simply say,
"Summer, oh, Summer,
come out and play."